Aella Greene

Rhymes of Yankee Land

Aella Greene

Rhymes of Yankee Land

ISBN/EAN: 9783337391911

Printed in Europe, USA, Canada, Australia, Japan

Cover: Foto ©Andreas Hilbeck / pixelio.de

More available books at **www.hansebooks.com**

RHYMES

OF

YANKEE LAND.

BY

AELLA GREENE.

———◆———

SPRINGFIELD, MASS.:

WHITNEY & ADAMS.

1872.

SAMUEL BOWLES & COMPANY,
PRINTERS, BINDERS, AND ELECTROTYPERS,
SPRINGFIELD, MASS.

TO

MY NEW ENGLAND FRIENDS,

AT HOME AND WESTWARD,

I Dedicate

THESE

"RHYMES OF YANKEE LAND."

CONTENTS.

THE

SMITHVILLE WORTHIES.

SQUIRE SMITH.

OLD Mister Smith of Smithville died
    Two weeks ago to-day ;
We always thought the person lied
    Who said he'd pass away.

With buoyant step, and fragrant breath,
    And face with health aglow,
He seemed no older near his death
    Than twenty years ago.

But gone he has, at last, from earth,
    As every mortal must,
Of noble or of lowly birth,
    Unrighteous they, or just.

Though it may seem as useless quite,
  To weep and make ado,
Still, I have thought it well to write
  Of him a rhyme or two.

Possessing not a noted name,
  Nor piles of treasure high,
He yet enjoyed of pelf and fame
  A moderate supply.

For comely speech, and good intent,
  And for his neat attire,
The villagers with one consent,
  Regarded him as "Square."

Attending church on Sabbath days,
  As everybody should,

He joined in all the prayer and praise,
　As pious people would.

Within the week he walked down town,
　On pleasant afternoons,
Wearing a modest suit of brown,
　And humming quiet tunes.

He kept his temper all the while,
　In weather dry or wet;
And had a penny, or a smile,
　For every child he met.

Of joy his heart the source and spring,
　To him no dark nor wrong;
He seemed from bitterest grief to bring
　The melody of song.

At inns he never lingered much,
　For beer and greater grog;
When coming home from clubs and such,
　Was never in a fog.

The Squire no stated calling had,
　A "jack at every trade;"
At neither one was reckoned bad,
　But quite a figure made.

Three years a farmer's life he led;
　There seemed to him a charm,
To gain his raiment and his bread,
　By managing a farm.

For several years he kept a school,
　In an adjoining place;

Maintaining there a pleasant rule,
  With dignity and grace.

He also wrote a little book
  About his native town,
That had a literary look,—
  Done up in covers brown.

To Washington he never went,
  As statesman had no forte ;
Yet twice had been as juror sent,
  And once to General Court !

He did not take to allopaths,
  As would some other men,
But patronized cold water baths,
  And sometimes took cayenne.

He spurned a miser as a thief,
And acted, "on the square;"
Though not a Mason, my belief
Is Smith had once been there.

He kept his courage always up,
And kept his record clear;
Kept only water in his cup,
And kept his wife so dear.

He kept of Sabbaths fifty-two;
Kept everything of worth;
Kept more than most of people do,
And always kept "the Fourth."

He kept his course with ease and grit;
Kept all he thought or heard,

That was for keeping really fit;

    And always kept his word.

Smith led a quiet, even life,

    And died at seventy-four;

Leaving to mourn him his good wife,

    And grown up children four.

And on that saddest funeral day,

    There gathered at his bier,

A thousand friends, as true and tried,

    As ever shed a tear.

Within the churchyard, 'neath a yew,

    They made his grave with care;

And lingeringly they bade adieu,

    With sorrow, and with prayer.

Ye better bards, to whom belong
High themes and lofty verse,
Still deem as not unworthy song,
The life these lines rehearse.

Although a humble man was he,
Our Smith was still a man;
As good on earth we seldom see,
And better, never can.

DOCTOR BLISS.

THE people were so seldom sick
   That it was very true,
The one physician in the town
   Had not enough to do.

This doctor was a gentleman,
   Of average grace and wit,
Who studied just six years, until
   For practice fully fit.

Then took his "sheep-skin" and his leave,
   And unto Smithville went,
There hung his shingle out, and lived
   Until his days were spent.

2

Although an allopath, he felt

    Not very much inclined,

To be at odds with those who had

    A different course in mind.

Indulging patients in their whims,

    He seldom would refuse

Such mild "botanics" as their friends

    Might deem it best to use.

He was so kind, this Doctor Bliss,

    To press him there to stay,

The townsmen all agreed by vote,

    A salary to pay.

That potent medicine, a smile,

    He carried everywhere,

To cheer the sick, and drive away
    That worst of curses, care.

A wit declared, and it was true,
    When sickness was about,
The doctor, walking through the town,
    Could *look the sickness out.*

There is a legend wide extant,
    Once Death came walking by,
The doctor challenged him to fight
    And made the monster fly.

But Bliss, devoted to the art
    Of making people well,
To sickness and to medicine,
    At last, a victim fell.

He loved the Squire, and looked like him,

    Clad trim in brown attire ;

Near him he lived, and now at death,

    Is buried near the Squire.

THE VILLAGE SCHOOL-MASTER.

A WORTHY gentleman in town,
    Respected and revered,
Was William Wilson, learned and wise,
    A teacher born and reared.

He was a very proper man,
    Yet cheerful as was meet;
None were more knowing in the place,
    Nor any so discreet.

The little school-house where he taught
    For twenty years and more,
Had but three windows on a side,
    And one above the door.

It cost six hundred dollars, just,
    As records do appear;
And yet the scholars came to think
    The place was very dear.

It stood upon the village green,
    Hard by the "center church;"
Was well supplied with furniture,
    But unsupplied with birch.

This Wilson had a better way
    To punish recreant boys,
Who had been lazy at their books,
    Or making needless noise.

Within a very "dreadful book,"
    Where every crime had grade;

For every wrong a scholar did,

   So many checks were made.

These famous checks had come to be

   Regarded with such dread,

Some of the culprits thought it were

   Far better to be dead.

With patience and with kindly care,

   He led his pupils through

The path of common learning, till

   They every feature knew.

And oft, perchance, they caught a glimpse

   Of classic grove and field,

And felt a longing for the fruits

   Those pleasant regions yield;

But Euclid and "the languages,"

   In district schools of yore,

Were all discarded and forbid,

   As very useless lore.

Since Wilson gave up teaching school,

   Ten years and five have passed ;

But through a century to come

   His influence shall last.

He still resides within the town ;

   And though threescore and ten,

The people all declare he is

   The comeliest of men.

CRISPIN CRANE.

IN praise of one whose worth and wit
  The Smithville people prize ;
Who, by a timely repartee,
  Found favor in their eyes :

Disciple of St. Crispin he,
  And christened Crispin Crane,
He mended boots and shoes for folks,
  To get his bread and gain.

A kind, a brave, a little man,
  But five feet tall when up,
He booted well each man that came,
  And then would ask to sup.

His dwelling was adjacent to
　His little shop, you see;
So, often, did his customers
　"Drop in" to take some tea.

He took their measure in the shop;
　When guests, they came to find
He fully had the power to take
　The measure of their mind.

Full often, in the village store,
　A brainless, brassy brag,
Did all the village people bore,
　Defeating wise and wag.

The townsmen said, "If any man
　Will squelch that dolt and fool,

We'll send him to the capitol,

Or fee his son at school."

One eve he boasted loud how great

His understanding was ;

" Let him among you show such mind,

A greater mind who has ! "

Said Crane—and pointed to his feet—

" Your 'standings large ! forsooth ;

None may gainsay the fact, for I

The measure took of both."

Annihilation is no name

For how that fellow felt ;

He hasted out and little boys

With pebbles him did pelt.

The morrow was town-meeting day,
 And ere the time was spent,
They voted all that Crane should be
 To legislature sent.

He proved so wise a little man,
 So jolly with his friends,
So loth to speak, and always, then,
 To bring about good ends,

So keen, and quick, and powerful, too,
 A boasting man to floor;
Some of the members of the House,
 I think about a score,

Drew up a paper in due form,
 And set it to their "fist,"

Of which, if records are correct,

    The following is the gist:

"Good Mister Smith, respected Squire,

    And friend of Crispin Crane;

We wish, at your election, you

    Would send him here again."

He went again, and still once more,

    Until six times in all;

Nor by the lures of lobby men

    Did he from honor fall.

'Twas in his time of public life

    A party rose and fell,

Whose bad disaster at their schemes

    'Tis pleasurable to tell.

Late in the term a question rose
   This party called the test;
For which their leader spoke at length,
   With artificial zest;

And wound his closing period up
   To show "How blessed the land,
When 'garjuns' of the public peace
   Labor reformers stand!"

"Labor reformers!" Crispin quoth,
   "That means too proud to work!
And rightly named, for well you like
   Life's burdens all to shirk.

"You're all adventurers and shams,
   Unknown to honest toil,

Full frequent at the village inns,

    And in the cheaper broils.

"Below the wrath of common men,

    Too cheap for ours by half,

We'll not oppose your plannings, but

    Explode them with a laugh!"

The wit that beamed in Crispin's eyes

    Put all in merry mood,

As rang around the galleries

    One soul-refreshing "Good!"

The gavel man forgot to rap,

    Reporters dropped their notes,

Some member moved "the question!" and

    It got a dozen votes.

And that's the way the party died

By this sarcastic Crane ;

And hence the reason he was sent

To General Court again.

And since he finished there for all,

And closed his public life,

He's just as busy in his shop

, And pleasant to his wife.

When once as petit juror drawn,

Crane went to county court,

To find how much the panel work

Was his delight and forte.

The court was held in meager hall,

Quite hot on summer days,

And in its age so trembling weak

'Twas fastened up by stays.

The judge who ruled that county court

Had good judicial grace;

He spoke melodiously, but wore

A stern, though sunny, face.

Serenely beamed through glasses bright,

The long-tried county clerk ;

Who able seemed for many years

To swear men into work.

Across the court room from his chair

Crane saw, in buff and blue,

The sheriff sit in dignity,

A pleasant man to view.

3

To try a foolish case about
    The matter of a "V,"
It cost a hundred dollars, just,
    Besides the lawyers' fee.

The "great case" of the term was next
    Before Crane's panel brought,
In which a citizen his claims
    Of railway people sought.

The wooden witnesses were turned
    By crafty lawyers round,
And made to swear that light was dark,
    And broken cars were sound.

The lawyers, next, their arguments
    Unto his honor spoke ;

And in their speech most fearfully
　　The ninth commandment broke.

The proper judge, polite and prompt,
　　The jurors charged full clear ;
And they a verdict gave, unbought
　　By favor, love, or fear.

It didn't suit defendants much ;
　　To make a greater stench,
They vowed to carry up the case
　　Unto the fuller bench.

One afternoon there came a lull,
　　In business of the court,
As lazy lawyers couldn't get
　　Their clients to report.

The judge evinced a wish to quit,
And bade to end the assize ;
" For when there is no work to do,
This court had better rise."

The crier closed the court, and said,
" God save the Commonwealth ! "
Opposing lawyers parted friends,
And wished each other health.

Crane's panel parted on the steps
Of that low, dingy hall,
With little hope it would give way
To comely building tall.

The public men who had in charge
The matter of a site,

Had passed their time in foolish fuss
    That grew into a fight.

That dingy court-house stands there still !
    A relic of the past ;
Wherein the lawyers show their wit,
    And argue questions vast.

MR. JONES, THE SMITH.

A STALWART, strong and cheerful man,
   Our village Vulcan, Jones,
Was no exception to the rule
   That smiths are seldom drones.
From morning stars till evening dews
   His swinging hammer rang,
In keeping with the words and tunes
   Of ballads which he sang.

Around his shop tall maples grew
   And robins caroled there,
And rose and daffodil exhaled
   Their sweetness on the air.

The gladdest man in town, he saw

More sadness than the rest, .

But found his joy in frequent work

To have the saddened blest.

The humbler people of the place

Esteemed him very dear ;

And men of higher rank than Jones

Have sought his shop for cheer.

Did any speak of loss, he showed

The faith which never tires ;

Or tell of luck, his face would glow

As ruddy as his fires.

And men who shine as millionaires

And rulers in the land,

Are glad to say, that, years ago,

    He gave a helping hand,

And spoke the words of cheer that gave

    Them courage for the fight,

And patience, as they watched through dark

    The coming of the light.

He seeks no higher station than

    His anvil and his home;

But neighbors think he'll have high place

    In that good world to come.

His life, throughout, an argument

    How grand the humble man,

In meekness who performeth all

    The noble deeds he can.

ABIJAH BEERS.

THOUGH Smithville was so blest of heaven,
To it one tedious thorn was given.
The place had one perfected sinner,
Most surely who had been the winner,
Did he and Satan run a race
On any course away from grace.
Supremely mean in all his deeds;
His heart as hard as flint; the needs
Caused by his extortions moved him not,
The pining poor were all forgot;
Selfish, thick, marble-faced and stern,
Full quick to sin, and apt to learn
The ways of avarice and wrong;

On primal sin improving long,

He chose oppression for his art,

And practiced it with all his heart;

His sinning cloaked with graciousness,

And cursed when he appeared to bless.

He so gifted in causing tears

Had fitting name, Abijah Beers.

May gods protect if here, again,

So bad a man 'mong living men;

And there was not, since earth began,

So much of meanness in a man.

The liberals declared for hell,

Else where could that sinner dwell.

He died at last as fools do die;

Thistles thrive where his ashes lie!

LIGHT FROM DARK.

INTO THE SUNSHINE.

COME to the sunshine bringing bloom,

    For the rose there's always room ;

Come to the sunshine bringing bloom.

Out from darkness and from night

Into the beams of morning light,

Out from darkness and from night.

Into the sunshine for relief,

Bring the troubled sons of grief ;

Into the sunshine for relief.

Into the sunshine with a song,

Grasp their hand and lead them strong

Into the sunshine with a song.

Bring to the sunshine of your trust;

If they succeed, you surely must

Bestow the sunshine of your trust.

Full and free, to all impart

The sunshine of a generous heart;

Full and free to all impart.

Live in the sunshine while you live,

And unto all your sunshine give;

Live in the sunshine while you live.

Into the sunshine when you die,

Into the sunshine up to the sky;

Into the sunshine when you die.

REST IN WORK.

OH, tell me some secluded place,
Where, weary with this fitful race,
These tired limbs awhile may rest,
These tired eyes with sleep be blest,
This aching heart be freed from cares,
From disappointments and despairs,
And breathe there o'er my soul a calm,
Amid the fragrance and the balm.

Yet, if it be not wise to rest;
If calls the race for speed and zest,
Or shine the fields with harvest white
That must be garnered ere the night,

My feet shall run, my hands shall toil,

No sighs for rest my purpose foil

To do the work and do it well.

No friends so fair or foes so fell

Shall win or fright me from the task,

Nor lessening of the work I'll ask.

I'll bear a manly part in life,

Nor fret or falter in the strife ;

And, spirit crushed or heart depressed,

Yet full of hope, alive with zest,

Protract youth's joys far into age,

Walk royally on pilgrimage ;

Be meek, but not a dolt nor slave ;

Patient in dole, in danger brave ;

'Till, blossomed white with grief or joy,

I take my bliss without alloy.

But tell me some sweet resting-place,

That I may better run the race ;

A respite give awhile from pain,

That I the grief may bear again.

Yet if this boon be still denied,

Oh ! Thou to whom none fruitless cried,

Grant me at least one sweet relief ;

Since there are ever sons of grief,

Grant me to help them bear the load

And teach to tread the paths I trod ;

In sympathy with those who weep

A respite from my sorrows reap.

4

"YEA, WELCOME GRIEF."

YEA, welcome grief in every form,—
  Of biting blast or whelming storm;
The streams that would an ocean fill,
Or slow, continuous, wearing rill;
Or trouble's flail, or sorrow's mill;
A thorny path up rocky hill,
Or desert sands to scorch the feet,
Where torrid suns in fervor beat;
Or barren, drear, and sunless plains,
Where gloomy winter monarch reigns.

Up rocky hills sweet arbors are,
And not a flaming sword to bar;

And shineth still, though still afar,

Hope's blessed, bright, benignant star.

Hot deserts their oases have;

And, crossed, the pleasant plash of wave,

And sound of brooks, and warbling grove,

Shall lift the pilgrim's heart above.

The true man says, though die I must,

Till death I'll keep a beaming trust,

Though every plan should fall in dust,

And choicest treasures yield to rust.

Night brings the day, grief bringeth bliss;

And never that but cometh this.

Peace follows war, thorns speak the rose;

Fatigue foreruns a sweet repose;

And he who toils, nor seeks for rest,

With respite from his work is blest.

Or this the doctrine of true saints,

That he who hath but patient plaints,

And interludes his woe with songs,

To royal race and home belongs;

And, crowned, shall come in little time

To thrones, and feast, and heavenly chime;

And gain within this earthly clime,

A joy above all harp and rhyme!

"HOW BLESSED AND TRUE THE BELIEF."

HOW blessed and true the belief,

That the joy which comes after grief

Is sweeter, and never so brief

As other joys.

How grandly inspiring the thought,

That the bliss by bitterness bought,

Is nearer to heaven than aught

On earth beside.

How sweet after storm is the sun,

And rest after labor is done,—

The peace that by battling is won,

And wealth, by toil.

If discouraged and distressed,
With sorrow and with care oppressed,
And sins confessed and unconfessed,
And every ill,

The heart were struggling for relief,
And found no succor from its grief,
In buoyant trust and bright belief—
How sad the earth.

But rules converse of these obtain,
Nor mortal suffered yet in vain,
A trivial nor the largest pain,
Nor ever will.

So let the troubled take good heart,
Learn well of suffering the art,

Nor shun to share a generous part

    In life's good griefs.

Right where unkindest luck o'ertakes,

Our happy planning rudely breaks,

Of choicest treasures havoc makes,

    We shall succeed.

We shall succeed, for God ordains,

Whoever suffers loss or pains,

Shall reap therefor abundant gains,

    The interest due.

Of none the Father has such care,

As those who have abundant share

Of losses and of griefs to bear,

    And foes to meet.

"THE SUGAR CAMP IN EARLY SPRING."

THE sugar camp, in early spring,
    Was fragrant 'neath the hill;
Where liquid sweet, from maple trees,
    Did pleasantly distill.

Beneath the slab-roofed shed the fires,
    O'er which the kettles hung,
And when the syrup "grained" in time
    The cranes were outward swung;

Then "dips" of waxen sugar, John,
    You offered to the girls,
Two smiling dears of sweet sixteen,
    With innocence and curls.

"THE SUGAR CAMP IN EARLY SPRING."

One was a sister, good and true,
    The other choicer friend,
Whom afterwards you vowed to love,
    Till earthly days should end.

And now the kerchief that she hemmed
    Is moist with tears you shed,
To think that ere the wedding day
    Your bonnie Jane was dead.

And so you sigh, and so you learn
    It is how sadly true,
Our choicest good and dearest friend
    Do quickly fade from view.

But every day you live to mourn
    You seem so much a man,

I am inclined to think the loss
　　Is other than a ban.

And yet 'tis tender business this,
　　To rightly touch the heart,
Which even long ago was called
　　From troth or kin to part.

MISCELLANEOUS.

MY COMRADE'S GRAVE.

A CHRISTIAN, comrade, son, and friend *
   Is slumbering 'neath this sod;
His form is there, his name with us,
   His spirit with his God.

Fit place it is for hero's grave,
   Where mountain zephyrs play;
Where fair ones bring the choicest flowers,
   And good men pause to pray.

To designate his sepulcher,
   We raise this shaft, but trust
His deeds shall live when monuments
   Are crumbled into dust.

             * John J. Bisbee, of Worthington.

A TRIBUTE.

KIND, Christian lady, faithful friend,
   Accept each humble line,
Inscribed, in heartfelt praise, to worth
   And noble deeds like thine.

How wise thy words, and fitly said ;
   They guide, encourage, cheer ;
Dispel the darkness of defeat,
   With hope displacing fear.

Some kindnesses are burdensome,
   In fact, designed as debts ;
Not thine, these favors, which, increased,
   But multiply regrets.

Like showers thy benedictions come,

    Refreshing as the dew ;

Delightful as the morning sun,

    Or as the upper blue.

Ah ! gentle friend, how bright the earth

    In every clime would be,

Did all admire and practice, too,

    Unselfishness like thee.

THE SWEETHEART.

SO bold, should one of you accuse

That some sweet girl inspires my muse,

To all the rest it would be news,

But not to me.

She never tells the blessed fact,

By any word or any act,

Evincing such consummate tact,

To keep it hid

She is not reckoned on the list,

Of those who try to "keep it whist;"

And in the search she might assist,

And no one guess.

We'll keep the secret a little more,

Then, as so many have before,

We'll seek the parson's friendly door,

And tell it there.

5

A MODEL SUNDAY-SCHOOL.

A SUNDAY-SCHOOL our special charge,
Wherein the little and the large,
Shall sweetest truths of gospel learn;
Do greatest work, nor smallest spurn;
But deem it ever grandest lot,
To gather in from hall and cot,
From way-side stroll, or nursery door,
The children of the rich and poor,
And teach them from the gospel word
The record of the blessed Lord,
Who came to earth, and took our dust,
And died to give us chance to trust.
No bashful boy without our door,

Shall weep that no one prizes more,

Nor asks to have a place within

The walls designed to fence out sin.

We welcome each, and welcome all,

And at the joy-inspiring call,

Of Sabbath bell, on Sabbath morn,

When brightest smiles his face adorn,

And at the eve, and through the week,

Each teacher will for learners seek,

And seek them gladly, grandly, too,

As angels highest errands do.

WHEN YOU AND I WERE BOYS.

WE count above our common good,
　　Selectest of our joys,
What people did in sunny times,
　　When you and I were boys.

'Mid lilacs and the clover bloom,
　　Our early moments ran ;
And happy in the songs of birds,
　　We journeyed up to man.

These scenes so blest to realize,
　　Are brighter, brighter far,
That memory doth with golden key
　　The gates of light unbar.

What other cure the world prescribes,
  By far the safest, best,
Is glancing at our early days,
  Is retrospect and rest.

From cares and crowds of urban life,
  From traffic of the town ;
From wearing toil in dust and din,
  From griefs that weigh you down ;

From present ill, and future dread,
  And all that fetters thee,
Come to the country and the past,
  Be innocent and free.

Review the scenes of early days,
  With kind, religious care ;

The neighborhood once all your world,
　　And every object there.

The pansied yard, the slant well-sweep,
　　And apple orchard near;
The ancient farm-house, broad and red,
　　By many memories dear;

The hay-field and the pasture wide,
　　The fences by the lane;
The thick-leafed maples where you hid
　　When pattered down the rain;

The road where erst the stage-coach ran,
　　You studied as it passed;
That yellow coach with "thorough-brace,"
　　And built to have it last;

The level and the hilly road,
  On which you trudged to school,
To "make your manners" and to learn
  Hard Colburn's sum and rule;

The school-house with its seats and stove,
  And desks where jack-knives wrought,
And all the friendships that arose
  'Twixt teacher and the taught;

The ancient church and man of prayer,
  And gracious words and looks;
The lessons of the Sunday class,
  And pleasant Sunday books—

These, and the thousand other scenes
  Thine early being knew

Shall bring thee blessed light and balm,

And keep thee fresh and true.

By frequently reviewing them,

Thou shalt be young till death

Shall lift thee to the rarer bliss

Of everlasting breath.

THE YANKEE WESTWARD.

IN every western state they are,
 True sons of Yankee land,
With earnest heart and buoyant hopes,
 And ready, skillful hand ;

With native wit and lore of books,
 Clear fire and common sense ;
With grit and patience to endure
 And earnestness intense.

They go with lasting faith and pluck,
 A freshness, and a trust,
They kept alive when erst they laid
 The Briton in the dust ;

To fell the forest and to build
   The railway and the mill;
A pilgrim school in every glen,
   A church on every hill;

To fence and till in yeoman farms,
   The prairie and ravine,
And build smart cities, in the wilds
   Where Indian foot hath been.

They go to win a lasting name
   For Yankees and the right,
And show to "redskin," Dutch and Celt,
   Their shrewdness and their might;

To utilize the beautiful,
   The useful beautify;

The toiler's station, and his work,
  With art to dignify.

They go to win achievements grand
  In all the arts of peace,
And lead the van of progress, till
  Time's course at last shall cease.

Fear not that in this boundlessness
  The Yankee will be lost,
Though not the farthest western wild
  But his sure foot hath crossed.

All that is sacred, fresh, or strong,
  In Plymouth Rock and shore,
Transplanted in the widening West,
  Shall live for evermore.

And so, Utopia realized,

Our land shall be adored,

Till all the kingdoms of the earth,

Are kingdoms of the Lord.

THE CRITICS.

THE wicked wish some critics have,
    And knack, and greed, to kill
May pass quite readily·for taste,
    And evidence of skill;

But were there none to write a rhyme,
    Or paragraph of prose,
How critics then would pass their time,
    Is more than mortal knows.

They might ascend the upper spheres
    And criticise the stars,
And teach good manners and good sense
    To Jupiter and Mars;

Then clip away old Saturn's rings

　　And set him bounds to run ;

Or venture near the solar fires

　　To regulate the sun.

And should these critics go to Heaven,

　　Their joy would be to tell

How saints might tune their harps correct,

　　Or sing hosannas well !

CHICAGO'S TRIAL BY FIRE.

THE proudest city of the West
    In desolation laid,
Chicago mourns her fortunes burned,
    Like gossamer they fade.
The meager cot, the grand hotel,
    The depot and exchange,
Are swept within the marching flame,
    Whose onward maddening range

Devours a league of marble wealth,
    And brings to naught the great,
At yester-eve who sat apart,
    Ensconced in princely state ;

And, musing on their large success,

Planned larger wealth to gain ;

But learn so soon, how sadly true,

That human hopes are vain.

Men of all stations hurry forth,

Rank now a thing unknown,

And 'scape, if so the flames permit,

The fiery, widening, zone,

Whose devastating sweep doth blot

The grandest works of men ;

As though the ancient Sodom scourge

Had rained on earth again.

Large pity for the desolate,

And reverence for God,

Are lessons of this ordeal

    As spreads the news abroad.

Then pour your wealth and comforts in

    To mend the losses made,

And ask the Lord to bid the fire,

    "Let, here, thy waves be stayed."

God's judgments are inscrutable,

    But wisely all designed;

Or fire, or flood, or pestilence,

    Or devastating wind.

And grand the city shall arise

    From ruins of to-day;

And, in the future of the land,

    Hold on its prosperous way.

Springfield, October 9, 1871.

6

"THE PAPER."

BE it the ponderous city print,
    Depicting urban ways,
With columns crowded with details
    Of enterprise and frays ;
Or, less pretentious and disturbed,
    The country weekly calm,
Delighting well the villagers
    With sentences like balm ;

It hath important mission, fraught
    With all that blesses earth,
And often maps the surest road
    To usefulness and worth.

It hath the ward of interests
  High, ever-during, great ;
Minute as little hamlets are,
  And wide as is the state.

The writer at his paragraphs,
  The printer working by ;
I pray their health and happiness
  May never come to "pi ; "
And that the sheet they print may live
  For many years to come,
Prepaid, respected, and the light
  Of rail-car, 'Change and home.